THIS COMIC
BELONGS TO:

Disney
Doc
McStuffins
TOY HOSPITAL

Published simultaneously in the United States and Canada by Joe Books Ltd,
489 College Street, Suite 203, Toronto, ON M6G 1A5

*www.joebooks.com*



First Joe Books edition: October 2017

Print ISBN: 978-1-77275-561-9
ebook ISBN: 978-1-77275-824-5



Library and Archives Canada Cataloguing in Publication
information is available upon request

Printed and bound in Canada
1 3 5 7 9 10 8 6 4 2

# Lambie and the McStuffins Babies

## CINESTORY COMIC

JOE BOOKS LTD

Meet Doc and Her Toys!
HALLIE IS THE JOLLY HEAD NURSE, WHO LIKES TO MAKE TOYS SMILE.
CHILLY IS THE HAPPY FACE THAT GREETS NEW PATIENTS.
DOC MCSTUFFINS IS THE HEAD OF MCSTUFFINS TOY HOSPITAL. SHE LOVES MAKING TOYS FEEL BETTER.
STUFFY IS IN CHARGE OF THE PET CLINIC.
LAMBIE IS THE SWEET, CARING HEAD OF THE NURSERY.

Disney
DOC McStuffins
TOY HOSPITAL
Created by Chris Nee
IT'S ANOTHER BUSY DAY AT THE TOY HOSPITAL NURSERY. LAMBIE IS DOING CHECKUPS.
YOUR CHECKUPS ARE ALMOST DONE. YES, THEY ARE!

THREE HEALTHY AND CUTITY-CUTE BABY DOLLS READY TO BE DELIVERED!
YOU CAN TAKE THEM TO THEIR NEW HOME THROUGH THE TOY BOX PORTAL.
I'LL HAVE *FOUR* MORE NEW DOLLS IN THE NURSERY BY THIS AFTERNOON!
I LOVITY-LOVE MY JOB!

HI, LAMBIE! HOW'S IT GOING?

HI, DOC! I WAS JUST GETTING THESE BLANKETS READY FOR THE NEW DELIVERY OF BABY DOLLS.
AS HEAD OF THE NURSERY, I'M ALWAYS READY!

EMERGENCY CALL FROM STUART STORK.
BEEP
HEY THERE, DOC. I WAS TRYIN' TO MAKE A RUSH DELIVERY.
I RUSHED TOO MUCH AND *TWISTED MY LEG!* I NEED A TOY DOCTOR.

DON'T WORRY, WE'RE ON OUR WAY!

BABY DOLL HEADQUARTERS? THE PLACE WHERE CUTITY-CUTE BABY TOYS ARE MADE?
THIS IS MY DREAMITY-DREAM COME TRUE!

RESCUE RONDA FLIES DOC AND THE TOYS OVER TOWN...
COOL!
WOW!

HERE WE ARE, BABY DOLL HEADQUARTERS.
THANKS RONDA.
TOYS, *LET'S* GO!

WELCOME!
I'M DELILAH, HEAD OF BABY DOLL HEADQUARTERS.
RIGHT THIS WAY!
I'VE NEVER SEEN SO MUCH CUTE IN ONE PLACE!

DELILAH LEADS DOC AND THE TOYS TO SEE STUART STORK.
DOC! YOU'RE HERE!
I DON'T THINK I CAN *WALK*, LET ALONE DELIVER BABIES.
LOOKS LIKE *YOU* NEED A CHECKUP.

DOC LISTENS TO STUART'S HEARTBEAT AND CHECKS HIS LEG.

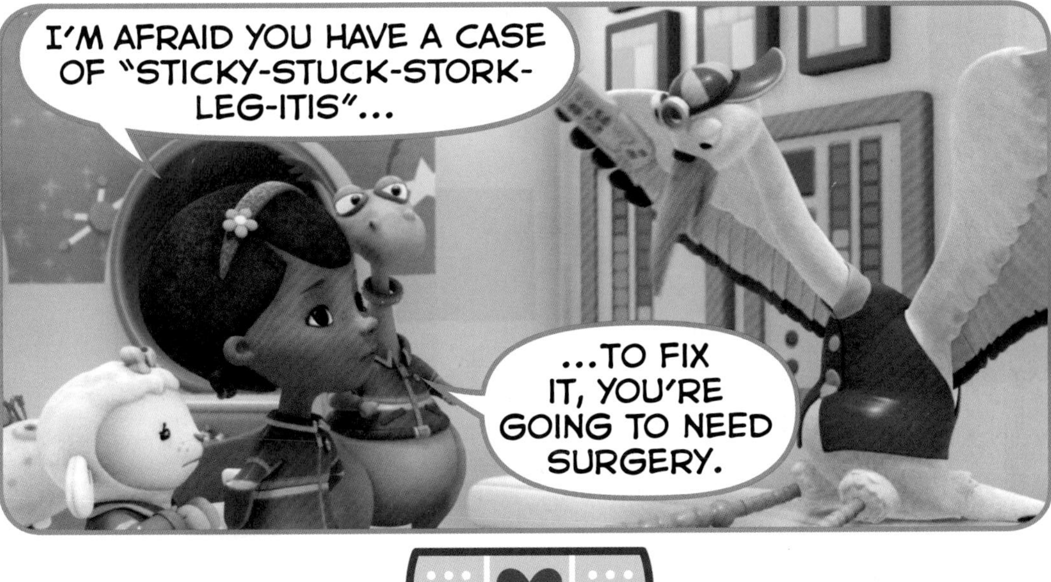
I'M AFRAID YOU HAVE A CASE OF "STICKY-STUCK-STORK-LEG-ITIS"...
...TO FIX IT, YOU'RE GOING TO NEED SURGERY.

IF I GO TO THE HOSPITAL, WHO'S GONNA MAKE MY DELIVERIES?
I WILL!
I'VE ALWAYS WANTED TO KNOW HOW BABY TOYS ARE DELIVERED!
PRETTY PLEASE, LET ME HELP!

STUFFY, CHILLY, AND HALLIE WANT TO HELP, TOO!

NOW *THAT'S* A STELLAR DELIVERY TEAM!
GOOD LUCK, GUYS.

DELILAH SHOWS THE TOYS TO THE GROUP OF BABY DOLLS THEY WILL BE DELIVERING.
THERE'S ONE MORE IMPORTANT STEP TO BRING THEM TO LIFE--*THE MAGIC HEART MAKER.*

IT TAKES THE MAGIC OF LOVE TO MAKE A BABY DOLL. THE MAGIC HEART MAKER IS FULL OF THAT MAGIC!
ONCE A DOLL RECEIVES A DOSE OF MAGIC, THEY'RE READY TO BE DELIVERED TO THE NURSERY.
BUMP
UH-OH! CHILLY IS ABOUT TO FALL OVER THE EDGE!

THE TOYS CATCH CHILLY, BUT HALLIE STARTS TO SLIP...
AHHHH!
BAAAAAA!!!
WOAAAH!
WHOOOOSH

ZING

OH NO! I BETTER CALL DOC!

WE'VE ALL TURNED INTO *BABY TOYS!!!*

WHAT JUST
HAPPENED?

THE OTHER BABY DOLLS ARRIVE.

WE MAY BE BABY TOYS, BUT WE MADE A *PROMISE* TO STUART.
WE'VE GOT TO GET THESE BABY DOLLS TO THE NURSERY FOR THEIR *CHECKUPS!*

THE TOYS ALL TUMBLE INTO ANOTHER SLIDE...
WHOOSH
PLONK
STUART'S BAG IS *STILL* HERE? I'D BETTER TAKE THIS ONE!

YIKES! THIS BAG IS HEAVY!
MR. STORK!!! DOWN HERE!
HE CAN'T HEAR US!
I WANT MY DOC-Y!!!

HOSPITAL OPERATING ROOM.
STORK SPLINT. THERE.
THAT SHOULD FIX STUART'S LEG.

DOC! LAMBIE, STUFFY, HALLIE, AND CHILLY FELL INTO THE MAGIC HEART MAKER! THEY'VE TURNED INTO BABY TOYS!
BEEP

OKAY. WE NEED TO SEND OUT AN EMERGENCY ALERT TO ALL STORKS ON DUTY!

BACK OVER THE FOREST...
BEEP BEEP BEEP
WOAAAAAAH! THE EMERGENCY ALERT!
THE ALERT STARTLES STEVIE STORK, AND THE DELIVERY BAG TIPS OVER...
AHHHH!

THE TOYS USE THE BAG AS A PARACHUTE...
...AND LAND SAFELY ON THE FOREST FLOOR.

OH, I PROMISED STUART I'D GET THE BABIES TO THE NURSERY...
WHAT ARE WE GONNA DO?
WE'RE GONNA FIND OUR WAY BACK TO THE HOSPITAL... *SOMEHOW.*

BACK AT THE HOSPITAL...
STEVIE, ANY NEWS?
BEEP
YOUR TOYS *WERE* IN MY BAG, DOC...BUT THEY FELL INTO THE WOODS! I CAN'T FIND THEM *ANYWHERE!*
KEEP LOOKING! I'M ON MY WAY.

IN THE FOREST...
THE HOSPITAL CAN'T BE *TOO* MUCH FARTHER. WE'LL KEEP GOING THIS WAY.
IT'S GETTING DARK. THE TOYS ARE SCARED AND UPSET.
WAAAA! WAHHH!
WWWROAR!
WAAHH!
27

DON'T CRY! SHHH, SHH.
IT'S OKAY...
THIS IS WORSE THAN MY BUSIEST DAY IN THE NURSERY!

WAIT...THIS IS *JUST* LIKE A DAY IN THE NURSERY.
IF I GIVE THE DOLLS A CHECKUP, EVERYONE MIGHT FEEL BETTER...

*LAMBIE LOOKS AFTER THE BABY DOLLS.*

THE TOYS HELP, TOO! EVERYONE FEELS BETTER AFTER A CUDDLE.

YOU HAVE A CASE OF "SLEEPY BABY SYNDROME." MY PRESCRIPTION IS ONE LAMBIE LULLABY...

THEY'RE ASLEEP.
NOW LET'S GET THEM TO THE NURSERY.

IN THE SKY ABOVE THE FOREST...
STEVIE WAS FLYING SOMEWHERE AROUND HERE.
I DON'T SEE ANY SIGN OF THEM!

HEY! DOWN HERE!
DOC!!!

IT'S TOO DARK! SHE DOESN'T SEE US!

MAYBE SHE'LL SEE THIS!

THERE THEY ARE!

WHAT'S GOING ON?
SPARKLES?

POOF!
WHERE ARE WE?

GASP! WE'VE BEEN DELIVERED TO A FAMILY!

I MUST HAVE PRESSED THE WRONG BUTTON ON STUART'S DEVICE!
I-I LET YOU DOWN...
YOU'VE BEEN KEEPING US GOING! WE'RE IN GOOD HANDS WHEREVER WE ARE...AS LONG AS WE'RE WITH YOU.

I'D DO ANYTHING FOR THESE DOLLS...AND MY FRIENDS.
THE TOYS HEAR FOOTSTEPS...
SOMEBODY'S COMING. QUICK! STUFF IT BABY-STYLE!
THUMP THUMP

WE CAN THROW THEM IN THE GOODIE BAG FOR ALL THE KIDS.
LET'S GET THE WRAPPING PAPER.

BACK AT THE HOSPITAL...
ROBOT RAY! FIRE UP THE SYSTEM! MY TOYS ARE OUT THERE SOMEWHERE.

COMMENCING TRACKING DEVICE.
I HOPE WE CAN FIND THEM.

BACK AT THE FAMILY'S HOUSE...
WE NEED TO FIND A TOY BOX! IT'LL LEAD TO THE HOSPITAL!
LET'S CHECK UPSTAIRS!

THE TOYS MAKE THEIR WAY TO THE STAIRS.

HE GOT MY BABY CARROT NOSE! I NEED A CHECKUP! *HELP!!!*

AT THE HOSPITAL...
HURT TOY ALERT. A BABY SNOWMAN HAS CALLED FOR HELP.
IT MUST BE CHILLY! TRY TO FIND HIM!

THE TOYS HEAD TOWARD THE CHILDREN'S ROOM.
WE'RE ALMOST THERE, LITTLE ONES.
LAMBIE LOVES YOU SO MUCH.

IT'S THE TOYS! THEY'RE HEADING FOR THE TOY BOX!

HURRY, LAMBIE!
NOT WITHOUT THE BABY DOLLS!
AT THE HOSPITAL...

YOU'RE HOME! AND SO...LITTLE.

I'M SO SORRY, DOC! I PROMISED YOU AND STUART I'D BRING THE BABY DOLLS TO THE NURSERY... BUT...I DIDN'T.
DON'T CRY, LAMBIE. LOOK!

THE BABY DOLLS ARE WHERE THEY BELONG.
AND *YOU* GOT THEM THERE SAFE AND SOUND.

BUT WHAT ABOUT THEIR CHECKUPS?
YOU GAVE THEM CHECKUPS, REMEMBER?

THAT'S WHY YOU'RE HEAD OF THE NURSERY.
YOU'RE GREAT WITH BABIES.

I'M HERE! I'M SO SORRY ABOUT THE MISHAP AT HEADQUARTERS.
I CAN REVERSE IT...WITH THIS!

ZING

YOU *WERE* REALLY CUTE BABIES!
BUT I'M GLAD YOU'RE BACK TO NORMAL.

NURSERY--THE NEXT DAY.
DELIVERY HERE!

STUART, THEY'RE BAA-EAUTIFUL... *AND* SLEEPY!
I KNOW JUST WHAT TO DO.

LAMBIE SINGS A LULLABY.

THEY'RE SO CUTE.

HA-HA! SO ARE THEY!
ZZZZZZZZZZZZZZZZZZZ

I GUESS I REALLY *AM* GOOD AT TAKING CARE OF BABY TOYS...*AND* MY FRIENDS!

**Lambie and the McStuffins Babies**

**Executive Producer and Story Editor**
Chris Nee

**Coexecutive Producer and Costory Editor**
Kent Redeker

**Executive Producers**
Cathal Gaffney
Darragh O'Connell

**Supervising Director and Consulting Producer**
Norton Virgien

**Written by**
Chelsea Beyl

CINESTORY COMIC

The Sleepover

CINESTORY COMIC

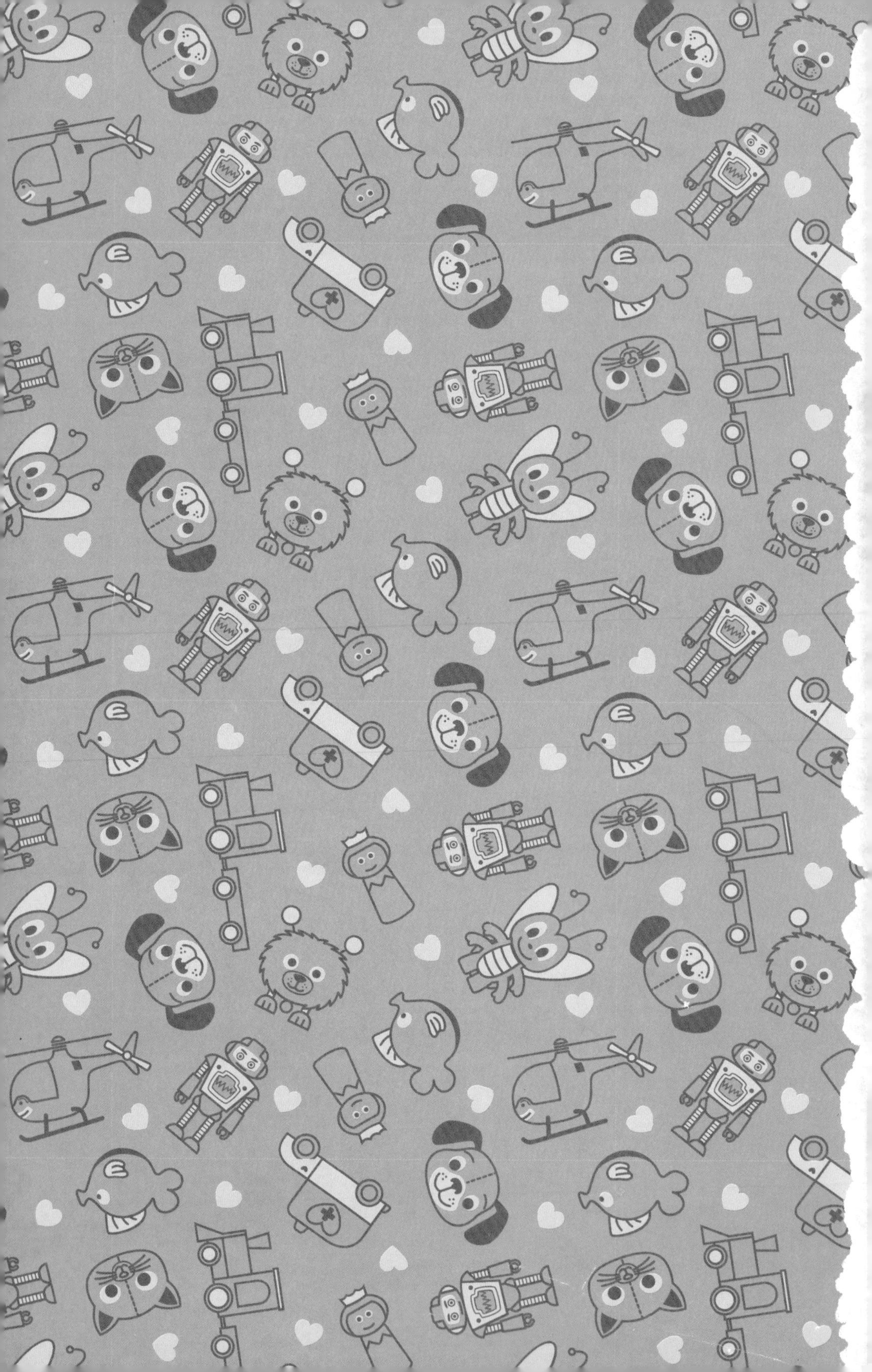